Wash, Wash, Wash

Grace Garrett

ISBN-13: 978-1491283066
ISBN-10: 1491283068

This book is dedicated to the wonderful and amazing MM'ers:
Karen, Melody, Pam, Susan and Vicki

Saul Samuel Slade loved to play.

He loved to run and
laugh all day.

After he played in his box of sand

his mom would tell him
to wash his hands.

"Wash, wash, wash your hands,"
she would say to Saul.

"Use soap and
wash, wash, wash
each finger, get them all."

Sometimes Saul would put his hands under the water

But just for a quick rinse before the water got hotter.

Other times he simply forgot
or was too busy.

He didn't have time to wait
for the soap to get fizzy.

He didn't wash, wash, wash his
hands unless his Mom was there.

He didn't use soap and
wash, wash, wash
each finger with care.

When he went to the bathroom
unless he was caught

he didn't stop to
wash, wash, wash his hands
like he had been taught.

He didn't wash, wash, wash his hands to get them clean.

He didn't wash, wash, wash them unless dirt could be seen.

Saul's mom warned him again and again not to be quick.

If he didn't wash, wash, wash his hands he could get sick.

Saul didn't listen, he just grinned.

He wouldn't get sick.
No indeed, not him.

But that's exactly what happened and at the worst time too!

Saul got sick the day his class was going to the zoo!

While the other kids got to see the lions and lambs

Saul was sick in bed because he didn't wash, wash, wash his hands.

Saul moaned, "If only I had wash, wash, washed my hands I wouldn't feel so bad."

"This is the worst sickness I've ever had!"

“This is worse than the chicken pox or the flu.”

“I can't believe I feel so blue!"

Saul was sick in bed
for a whole week.

He didn't get to go to
the zoo or play
or get any treats.

Saul learned his lesson
well that day.

Now he always
wash, wash, washes
his hands the right way.

He uses soap and water
every time

to wash, wash, wash away
all of the grime.

Even if he can't see the dirt he
knows it could be there

So he wash, wash, washes
his hands with great care.

Saul now says "Wash, wash, wash your hands just like me."

"Always use soap and water to keep them clean!"

The End

Made in the USA
Middletown, DE
02 October 2018